THE CHRISTMAS TREE FOREST

by

Raymond MacDonald Alden

Illustrated by Rafaello Busoni

There were many curious things about the Great Walled Country, but this story is only about the Christmas season there. All the inhabitants were children and they never grew up in this land of ice and snow. Grandfather Christmas always left his presents in the forest and the children sometimes were disappointed. One year a visitor climbed over the wall and persuaded the Child-King to change the Christmas custom so everyone would be better satisfied if he got presents just for himself. A little boy, Inge, knew his crippled sister couldn't go to the forest, so he broke the rule and brought back things only for her. The other children couldn't find any gifts. It was a Christmas the children never forgot, because they learned a valuable lesson about giving.

* *

Dewey Decimal Classification: Fic

About the Author:

RAYMOND MACDONALD ALDEN was a university professor of English, who wrote a great many books, most of them for grownups. The ones remembered now are the two he wrote for young people, *Why the Chimes Rang* and *The Boy Who Found the King*. His father was a minister and his mother, Isabella MacDonald Alden, wrote many books for young people, and for twenty-five years edited a juvenile magazine, *Pansy*. Mr. Alden was born in New York State, and taught at a number of universities. He was Director of the Drama League of America from its founding to 1914.

About the Illustrator:

RAFAELLO BUSONI began to draw before he was six and at eleven was given his first oil paint set. He had a one-man show of his paintings when he was seventeen. He was the son of a famous Italian pianist. He went to school in Germany, where he was born, then in Switzerland, and the United States. Mr. Busoni is skilled in all the graphic arts, but it was not until his son was old enough for books that he turned his attention to those for children. He has illustrated dozens of them, and has also written them. For a number of years he made more than two thousand drawings for film strips used in American schools.

THE
CHRISTMAS TREE
FOREST

By RAYMOND MacDONALD ALDEN

Illustrated by Rafaello Busoni

THE BOBBS-MERRILL COMPANY, INC.
Publishers

INDIANAPOLIS • NEW YORK

*A*WAY at the northern end of the world, farther than men have ever gone with their ships or their sleds, and where most people suppose that there is nothing but ice and snow, is a land full of children, called The Great Walled Country. This name is given because all around the country is a great wall, hundreds of feet thick and hundreds of feet high. It is made of ice, and never melts, winter or summer; and of course it is for this reason that more people have not discovered the place.

The land, as I said, is filled with children, for nobody
who lives there ever grows up. The king and the queen,
the princes and the courtiers, may be as old as you please,

but they are children for all that. They play a great deal
of the time with dolls and tin soldiers, and every night
at seven o'clock have a bowl of bread and milk and go

to bed. But they make excellent rulers, and the other children are well pleased.

There are all sorts of curious things about the way they live in The Great Walled Country, but this story is only of their Christmas season. One can imagine what a fine thing their Christmas must be, so near the North Pole, with ice and snow everywhere; but this is not all. Grandfather Christmas lives just on the north side of the country, so that his house leans against the great wall and would tip over if it were not for its support. Grandfather Christmas is his name in The Great Walled Country; no doubt we should call him Santa Claus here. At any rate, he is the same person, and be sure he loves the children behind the great wall of ice.

One very pleasant thing about having Grandfather Christmas for a neighbor is that in The Great Walled Country they never have to buy their Christmas presents. Every year, on the day before Christmas, before he makes up his bundles for the rest of the world, Grandfather Christmas goes into a great forest of Christmas

trees that grows just back of the palace of the king of
The Great Walled Country, and fills the trees with
candy and books and toys and all sorts of good things.
So when night comes, all the children wrap up snugly,

while the children in all other lands are waiting in their beds, and go to the forest to gather gifts for their friends. Each one goes by himself, so that none of his friends can see what he has gathered; and no one ever thinks of such a thing as taking a present for himself. The forest is so big that there is room for everyone to wander about without meeting the people from whom he has secrets, and there are always enough nice things to go around.

So Christmas time is a great holiday in that land, as it is in all the best places in the world. They have been celebrating it in this way for hundreds of years, and since Grandfather Christmas does not seem to grow old any faster than the children, they will probably do so for hundreds of years to come.

But there was once a time, so many years ago that they would have forgotten all about it if the story were not written in their Big Book and read to them every year, when the children in The Great Walled Country had a very strange Christmas. There came a visitor to the land. He was an old man, and was the first stranger for very many years who had succeeded in getting over the wall. He looked so wise, and was so much interested in what he saw and heard, that the king invited him to the palace, and he was treated with every possible honor.

When this old man had inquired about their Christ-

mas celebration, and was told how they carried it on every year, he listened gravely, and then, looking wiser than ever, he said to the king:

"That is all very well, but I should think that children who have Grandfather Christmas for a neighbor could find a better and easier way. You tell me that you

all go out on Christmas Eve to gather presents to give
to one another the next morning. Why take so much
trouble, and act in such a roundabout way? Why not
go out together, and everyone get his own presents?
That would save the trouble of dividing them again,
and everyone would be better satisfied, for he could pick
out just what he wanted for himself. No one can tell
what you want as well as you can."

This seemed to the king a very wise saying, and he called all his courtiers and counselors about him to hear it. The wise stranger talked further about his plan, and when he had finished they all agreed that they had been very foolish never to have thought of this simple way of getting their Christmas gifts.

"If we do this," they said, "no one can ever complain of what he has, or wish that someone had taken more pains to find what he wanted. We will make a proclamation, and always after this follow the new plan."

So the proclamation was made, and the plan seemed as wise to the children of the country as it had to the king and the counselors. Everyone had at some time been a little disappointed with his Christmas gifts; now there would be no danger of that.

On Christmas Eve they always had a meeting at the palace, and sang carols until the time for going to the forest. When the clock struck ten everyone said, "I wish you a Merry Christmas!" to the person nearest him, and then they separated to go their ways to the forest. On this particular night it seemed to the king that the music

was not quite so merry as usual, and that when the children spoke to one another their eyes did not shine as gladly as he had noticed them in other years; but there could be no good reason for this, since everyone was expecting a better time than usual. So he thought no more of it.

There was only one person at the palace that night who was not pleased with the new proclamation about the Christmas gifts. This was a little boy named Inge, who lived not far from the palace with his sister. Now his sister was a cripple, and had to sit all day looking out of the window from her chair; and Inge took care of her, and tried to make her life happy from morning till night. He had always gone to the forest on Christmas Eve and returned with his arms and pockets loaded with pretty things for his sister, which would keep her amused all the coming year. And although she was not able to go after presents for her brother, he did not mind that at all, especially as he had other friends who never forgot to divide their good things with him.

But now, said Inge to himself, what would his sister

do? For the king had ordered that no one should gather any presents except for himself, or any more than he could carry away at once. All of Inge's friends were busy planning what they would pick for themselves, but the poor crippled child could not go a step toward the forest. After thinking about it a long time, Inge decided that it would not be wrong if, instead of taking gifts for himself, he took them altogether for his sister. This he would be very glad to do; for what did a boy who could run about and play in the snow care for presents, compared with a little girl who could only sit still and watch others having a good time? Inge did not ask the advice of anyone, for he was a little afraid others would tell him he must not do it; but he silently made up his mind not to obey the proclamation.

And now the chimes had struck ten, and the children were making their way toward the forest in starlight that was so bright that it almost showed their shadows on the sparkling snow. As soon as they came to the edge of the forest, they separated, each one going by himself in the old way, though now there was really no reason why they should have secrets from one another.

Ten minutes later, if you had been in the forest, you might have seen the children standing in dismay with tears on their faces, and exclaiming that there had never been such a Christmas Eve before. For as they looked eagerly about them to the low-bending branches of the evergreen trees, they saw nothing hanging from them that could not be seen every day in the year. High and low they searched, wandering farther into the forest than ever before, lest Grandfather Christmas might have

chosen a new place this year for hanging his presents; but still no presents appeared. The king called his counselors about him and asked them if they knew whether anything of this kind had happened before, but they could tell him nothing. So no one could guess whether Grandfather Christmas had forgotten them, or whether some dreadful accident had kept him away.

As the children were trooping out of the forest, after hours of weary searching, some of them came upon little Inge, who carried over his shoulder a bag that seemed to be full to overflowing. When he saw them looking at him, he cried:

"Are they not beautiful things? I think Grandfather Christmas was never so good to us before."

"Why, what do you mean?" cried the children. "There are no presents in the forest."

"No presents!" said Inge. "I have my bag full of them." But he did not offer to show them, because he did not want the children to see that they were all for his little sister instead of for himself.

Then the children begged him to tell them in what

part of the forest he had found his presents, and he turned back and pointed to the place where he had been. "I left many more behind than I brought away," he said. "There they are! I can see some of the things shining on the trees even from here."

But when the children followed his footprints in the snow to the place where he had been, they still saw nothing on the trees, and thought that Inge must be walking in his sleep, and dreaming that he had found presents. Perhaps he had filled his bag with the cones from the evergreen trees.

On Christmas Day there was sadness all through The Great Walled Country. But those who came to the house of Inge and his sister saw plenty of books and dolls and beautiful toys piled up about the little cripple's chair; and when they asked where these things came from, they were told, "Why, from the Christmas tree forest!" And they shook their heads, not knowing what it could mean.

The king held a council in the palace and appointed a committee of his most faithful courtiers to visit Grandfather Christmas and see if they could find what was the matter. In a day or two more the committee set out on their journey. They had very hard work to climb the great wall of ice that lay between their country and the place where Grandfather Christmas lived, but at last they reached the top. And when they came to the other side of the wall, they were looking down into the top of his chimney. It was not hard to go down this chimney into the house, and when they reached the bottom of it they found themselves in the very room where Grandfather Christmas lay sound asleep.

It was hard enough to waken him, for he always slept one hundred days after his Christmas work was over, and it was only by turning the hands of the clock around two hundred times that the committee could do anything. When the clock had struck twelve times two hundred hours, Grandfather Christmas thought it was time for his nap to be over, and he sat up in bed, rubbing his eyes.

"Oh, sir!" cried the prince who was in charge of the committee, "we have come from the king of The Great Walled Country, who has sent us to ask why you forgot us this Christmas, and left no presents in the forest."

"No presents!" said Grandfather Christmas. "I never forget anything. The presents were there. You did

not see them, that's all."

But the children told him that they had searched long and carefully, and in the whole forest there had not

been found a thing that could be called a Christmas gift.

"Indeed!" said Grandfather Christmas. "And did little Inge, the boy with the crippled sister, find none?"

Then the committee was silent, for they had heard of the gifts at Inge's house, and did not know what to say about them.

"You had better go home," said Grandfather Christmas, who now began to realize that he had been awakened too soon, "and let me finish my nap. The presents were there, but they were never intended for children who were looking only for themselves. I am not surprised that you could not see them. Remember that not everything that wise travelers tell you is wise." And he turned over and went to sleep again.

The committee returned silently to The Great Walled Country, and told the king what they had heard. The king did not tell all the children of the land what Grandfather Christmas had said, but, when the next December came, he made another proclamation, bidding everyone to seek gifts for others, in the old way, in the Christmas tree forest. So that is what they have been doing ever since; and in order that they may not forget what happened, in case anyone should ever ask for another change, they have read to them every year from their Big Book the story of the time when they had no Christmas gifts.